Late Nights

Ain't No Rest For The Wicked, Volume 1

Ivy Ingle-Moss

Published by Ivy Ingle-Moss, 2024.

LATE NIGHTS

First edition. July 5, 2024.

ISBN: 979-8227237286

Written by Ivy Ingle-Moss.

Table of Contents

For all of you naughty minxes awake past your bedtime...

Chapter 1 - Finding TitanVideos

Madeline's wrists were sore from typing all day. Her head pounded from sitting beneath dull office lighting. She was in such a foul mood that she didn't know what she could do to make herself feel better and it was all Atlas Bentley's fault.

He was the most pompous, rich, arrogant sod on the planet but he thought himself the prince of the governmental cleric's office. He would bat down every idea she had without justification, interrupted her and generally embarrassed her in front of their boss, Councilman Gilbert, and thought himself so fucking attractive that he could get away with it. She could tell by the way he would run his hands through his blond hair and wink over to her after he'd get even one word of praise where she wouldn't.

Yes, he was objectively attractive. Aggravatingly so. But his personality was so repellent that she refused to let herself think of him in any way other than as her most untrusted rival. In fact, he was her only source of frustration in the office and she truly believed that she would have moved up the career ladder by now if he had never taken the position.

One of these days, she would get promoted above him and then he wouldn't laugh at her.

"I know what will make you feel better," her best friend and resident life coach Dahlia said as she pulled out the bar stool beside her, flicking her hair over her shoulder. They had come to The Lord's Fountain, London's newest pub, to let off some steam after a busy and stressful week.

Madeline would have preferred to be at home tucked up in bed with a book and a glass of wine. She was somewhat of a recluse, truth be told, and it was only at Dahlia's insistence that she ever really went anywhere that wasn't the office or her apartment.

"You should find a man, take him home and let him fuck you until you've forgotten your own name."

The woman always had such a way with words. Madeline rolled her eyes and took a sip from her over-full, and rightfully so, glass of red wine.

"I don't—" she sighed. "I don't need a shag, Lia. What I need is to be recognised by the Councilman for all of the overtime I'm doing on this project."

"Boring!" Dahlia declared and crossed her long, tanned and slender legs over each other. Madeline knew she had stopped listening the second her idea to just 'get fucked' was swept off the table. The woman was all sex and by the way she was looking around the bar, she had no intention of going home alone.

The two of them were truly day and night. Dahlia was the embodiment of sex and seduction - her knee-length black hair, full lips and curvy body gained the attention of both men and women. Whereas Madeline had always been short and petite, frizzy-haired and studious.

She was hardly anybody's wet dream.

"Fine, well if you won't let one of those sexy men over there take you home..." Dahlia pointed not-so discreetly to the edge of the bar where a few rugged-looking men were enjoying a drink. "Then at least look after yourself when you curl up under that infernal heated blanket of yours."

The insinuation that Madeline acted beyond her years wasn't lost on her but perhaps Dahlia was right. She couldn't remember the last time she allowed herself to run her hands over her own body to get off.

In fact, she couldn't remember when she'd last orgasmed at all. Her previous lovers weren't exactly studs, nor were they anything above average in terms of their ability to pleasure a woman. And most fundamentally to Madeline, they insisted she spend too much time with them. As though her career prospects, her hopes and dreams meant nothing. And she could be heartless when she needed to be, especially when they got in the way of her future plans, which meant that each relationship had come to an abrupt and sudden end.

Dahlia, on the other hand, seemed to enjoy the casual sex life she had. From failed relationship to failed relationship, Madeline had begun to see the merit in that. In getting what you want and then never seeing that person again. There would be no one vying for her attention, no cause to give up on her dreams to suit anybody else and it would always be on her terms.

But not tonight. Tonight, her eyes were sore with their mission to stay open and her bed was calling. She said a quick goodbye to Dahlia, asking her to send a message once she got home safe and caught a taxi back to her apartment.

Annoyingly, once she had arrived and settled into bed, Madeline couldn't stop tossing and turning. Her mind was too preoccupied thinking about what she would give in that moment to have a way to get off. She deserved it after the week she'd had. So she opened up her laptop and loaded OnlyFans, a site she had briefly visited before when she needed a little reprieve. She had given up on it last time however, when she couldn't find anything that caught her fancy.

Madeline was just about to pack it all in and decide to grab a hot chocolate instead that would hopefully send her to sleep when she stumbled upon something very intriguing.

With the speed with which she was scrolling through the site, she might have almost carried on past the blond's profile photo if his username hadn't also caught her attention. TitanVideos.

Titan: The heralding title given to the Greek God Atlas.

Great, so her colleague was even obnoxious online.

A wide smile stretched over her face as she thanked herself for having a passing interest in Greek mythology. Without it, she might never have found Atlas Bentley's OnlyFans account.

At first, she considered whether to click onto his profile. Would it breach some type of barrier? To be able to view naked photos of him? How would she be able to look him in the eye at work if she knew what his body looked like? If she knew what he got up to in his evenings for his subscribers?

Her curiosity got the better of her as she considered that she could always use it as blackmail if she ever needed to. The opportunity was bound to appear sooner or later and she would take great pleasure in using it if he carried on the way he was going. If she ever suffered another setback due to his tampering, she would use this late night activity of his against him. With that thought in mind, she clicked onto his profile photo and took a closer look but was surprised to find that he wore a skull and crossbones mask over his face. It intrigued her to say the least. Why bother? Surely part of the appeal was that people were able to see his handsome face. Piggish and bullheaded as he was, he was gorgeous to look at so why cover that up?

As she scrolled through his account, she saw that the majority of his posts were blocked, requesting that she subscribe if she wanted to see more. There was no way she was about to pass up the chance to get more information about his secret life and that's what she told herself as she entered her card details and became his five-thousandth subscriber.

All at once, his entire content history became available to her and she didn't know where to start. In the first few videos she consumed, the mask was nowhere to be seen and he merely played a video game dressed entirely in baggy black loungewear. That's when she tuned into the video he was making live, noticing that the ones she had watched were a little old, and her heart rate soared thinking that he was sitting at home, right at that moment with his camera pointed at him. The intimacy of it was intense but she needed to know more.

She failed to believe that five-thousand people would subscribe just to watch him play a game for a couple of hours. No way, there was no possible way that's all he did. Besides, she thought, if it was, wouldn't he put his content on another site?

The reason she had gone onto OnlyFans to satisfy a craving she had was to see some—

Oh.

"Wow."

The word had escaped her mouth involuntarily and she slammed her laptop lid shut, jumping away from it with such a haste as guilty feelings began to surface. She knew what she was getting herself into. She understood that if she kept on digging that she would find the exact reason he listed the word 'snake' as a descriptor for himself in his bio. But nothing had prepared her for the sight of his large, thick cock on full display.

After running to the kitchen to grab herself a drink and to splash her face with water to soothe her burning cheeks, Madeline returned to her bed. The laptop sat there on her satin sheets tempting her, taunting her to reopen it and she did.

She studied him in full detail, having zoomed in at the exact moment his hard cock had sprung out of his jogging pants. Madeline could hear her heartbeat pounding in her ears when she noticed the silver piercings that adorned the length of him, squeezing the thick vein that ran along it.

She thought she had seen a good variety of male appendages in her time - five wasn't too many nor too few - but *his* was the first to cause a shot of arousal to fire to her core just at the sight of him.

Tentatively, she proceeded to watch him wrap his hand around himself as though that wasn't a completely inappropriate thing to do. Considering the fact that she knew him, where his other subscribers didn't, she questioned her own morals when she didn't tear her eyes away.

Madeline watched him run one hand down his chest whilst the other pumped himself hard until his cock pulsed, his body stiffened and his cum coated his fingers at the same time that a masculine moan escaped his throat.

The thing that surprised her the most wasn't the size of his cock, however. Nor was it the tightness of his muscled body. It was how soft, breathy and deep his voice had become when he spoke to his viewers. She had never heard it be so gentle.

"Fuck, you guys make me so fucking hard. Who wants to lick this off?"

His accompanying laugh sounded so rough, like it had originated in the depths of his soul, and so sinful that her clit began to throb with all of the unresolved tension from her stressful week.

Who could it hurt if she was to dip her fingers beneath the band of her panties? Who would even know besides herself if she used his videos to bring herself to orgasm? The fact that he wore his mask, that pulled tight to his chiseled jawline and showed off his pronounced adam's apple, as he played with himself made it far easier for her to make the decision to join him in his masturbation.

That thin layer of material, that she could only see his silver-blue eyes through, created such a beautiful illusion in her mind of a sexy, broad and well-endowed man with the deepest and most erotic voice she'd ever heard. It wasn't Atlas Bentley that she was getting off to now. It was Titan.

And, Heaven help her, was he good at his job.

"So, what do you want to see next?" He asked his fans as streams of messages flooded his chat room. "Mm, the consensus is out on this one. I've never done this before but I'm nothing if not experimental."

The wink he gave to the camera made her eyelashes flutter and she dragged her pyjama shorts down her legs. Her panties followed as she prepared herself to watch whatever it was that his subscribers had voted to see.

Pushing his mask slightly up his face so that his full lips came into view, he smirked before sticking out his tongue and crudely licked his own release from his fingers. He sucked them into his mouth and spun his tongue around each digit until they were entirely clean.

He was filling her head with such dirty thoughts that her core began to clench around nothing, wishing to be filled by the cock she'd just witnessed pulse with his hot cum. Madeline wondered what his piercings would feel like as they brushed against her inner walls.

"You guys are a bad influence. I love you all so much," he smirked, sticking out his tongue to show that he'd swallowed it all, before pulling his mask back down his face.

He was positively filthy and every movement he made, every word to be uttered from his mouth pushed her closer and closer to an orgasm that was building so acutely on her senses that she knew it would feel like ecstasy.

She just needed a little more. Just something.

Madeline feared that she wouldn't get there though when he began to wrap up his show for the night.

"You're all so fucking filthy, thank you for helping me get off tonight. Make sure you tune in tomorrow to watch me do it all again. Oh, and thanks also to my newest subscriber, Bookworm97. I hope you enjoyed yourself, baby," he grumbled.

He pulled up his mask one last time and sucked his pointer finger into his mouth whilst staring directly into the camera. Directly at her, at Bookworm97, and she knew what he was saying.

Come.

Just then stars burst behind her closed lids, her back arched against her mattress and her fingers became sticky with her release as his seductive voice pushed her into a leg-shaking orgasm.

She didn't feel guilty one bit.

Chapter 2 - His Highest Tipper

Within six months, Madeline had worked her way up to become TitanVideo's most-watched subscriber.

She had memorised every single detail of Titan's body from the cute freckles that adorned his shoulders to the bold black tattoos that decorated his well-shaped muscles. The captivating snake tattoo with its fangs bared on his forearm was her particular favourite. It was so dark and deadly and made her want to run her fingers over every line.

It was safe to assume that she would tune in every night to watch his stream. She could hardly help herself, too curious to see what he would do next and she was never disappointed.

Madeline had orgasmed more times by her own hand whilst watching him than as a result of the ministrations any man had given her. Her lustful infatuation with the masked man was becoming obsessive, quite frankly, but she didn't see the harm in it. Nobody knew she was watching him and she'd taken Dahlia's advice, after all.

The woman had spotted the change in her best friend almost overnight. Madeline was generally in a better mood, she went out with Dahlia a little more often - well, only until Titan started his late night stream - and she complained about work a lot less frequently. Despite the fact that Atlas Bentley still pissed her off like nobody else.

He'd gone above and beyond in the last couple of months too, which she couldn't figure out the reason behind, as he'd actually sabotaged her team's campaign for the upcoming local election. Madeline had been working early mornings - rather than late so that she wouldn't miss a particular somebody's stream - to complete her work in good time too. All that hard work down the drain, all for her rival's benefit. To say the man gave zero shits about her, her progression and her commitment was an understatement and it was as though he got off on making her miserable. He was rude, ignorant and a general nightmare to deal with but at least she had Titan to look forward to when she got home.

'Tan', as she'd taken to nicknaming him in her own head and screaming as she came, was all she ever needed. That's why, not even a couple of months into watching him, she'd begun to tip him generously.

Very generously.

It had started when she'd noticed that Tan would speak directly to his tippers and would even take special requests from those who donated the most.

That's how she had gotten herself into the rather sticky situation of watching him tip double cream down himself with her fingers buried deep inside her slick pussy.

"Bookworm, this is all for you," he groaned as the cold liquid dripped down his hard cock.

She had never wanted to suck a man off more in her life and kept licking her lips as though he would jump through her laptop screen, pin her to her bed and fuck her throat until she was rendered near unconscious.

Oh, if there was anything Tan's stream had opened her eyes to, it was the number of repressed kinks she seemed to have. Before watching him, she had no interest in piercings particularly or of using food in the bedroom and she certainly had never thought about cum play before.

That had become an almost daily benefit at this point so she felt no guilt whatsoever to herself for having spent a good amount of her savings on the man. Nobody had ever made her feel so powerful and free. Not to mention the fact that she now would consider herself sex positive in every meaning of the phrase. Where before she was used to vanilla sex and that was fine, all things considered, she knew she could no longer return to it.

Now, she wanted nobody but Titan.

It was a cause for alarm, when she really thought about it, that the only person she wanted to touch her and fuck her was a fictional man that lived within her computer.

Except... he wasn't fictional, was he?

Whenever she'd think too deeply on it, that line between Atlas Bentley and Titan became harder to distinguish and the shame that she'd experience at the prospect that she was morbidly attracted to her rival was overwhelming. He'd poke fun at her during the day and do as she asked at night.

It was thrilling, in a way, that she had him under such a level of control like this. She pulled the strings. She decided if she wanted him to edge himself for her entertainment. She dictated whether he would fuck his hand or his fleshlight toy. And when she tipped him £200 to get his nipples pierced, she could have melted into her mattress when he appeared in his next stream with them sore and red.

The silver metallic balls that poked out beside each hardened bud practically put her in a trance when she first saw them and she'd tipped him the same amount that they had cost in gratitude.

It was okay, she reasoned, she didn't have a boyfriend and if she did, she would likely spend that money on the man in her life anyway. On holidays for the two of them or whatever else couples got up to together. Except she didn't want a man bringing her down or telling her what to do, unless in the bedroom, and she certainly didn't need a holiday. She was far too busy making strides, or trying to, within her career for any of that.

Tan made her happier than any man had before him. He was hot, responsive and, most importantly, on *her* terms.

To enjoy him, all she had to do was forget about his daylight alter ego. It was hard to do so when he made the evidence of his discomfort known however. On the day he'd gotten said nipple piercing, he had taken the morning off for his appointment. Unbeknownst to Madeline at the time. It was bliss in the office for those four short hours and she had thanked her lucky stars for the reprieve.

When she returned from her lunch break however, there he was. Rubbing his hands softly over his pectorals and wincing in pain. She could only laugh at Atlas but she would never laugh at Tan and that was the difference. The huge startling difference that she had to maintain, lest she lose her most favourite pastime; watching him touch himself until he came.

Somehow she managed it though. Call it her excessive imagination. She had always been able to throw herself into a story and picture herself the damsel in distress or warrior maiden. Here, the cards were just reversed, that was all.

It helped that he knew how to act. He would play and tease and flirt like Atlas Bentley never would. She didn't think he was even capable of it. In fact if he tried, she was sure it would come across sleazy and dirty instead. One cold September evening, she began her nightly ritual; dinner for one, a glass of wine and Titan for desert.

He started slowly and she always enjoyed it when he did. The build up was her favourite before she would ultimately ruin her sheets for him. Though this time, he was acting a little differently she noticed.

He would normally begin by welcoming all of his newest followers and asking them if they had any special requests. If nobody did, which was rare, he would go along with his own plan for the evening.

"Bookworm," he breathed into his mic. Madeline's core clenched immediately. "Tell me, baby, what do you want tonight? I've worked out that you're my highest tipper so this evening is for you."

A smile broke out on her face and she blushed. *Hard.* She always loved when he called her 'baby' or spoke directly to her at all. It was the entire reason that she was his highest tipper and the thought filled her with pride. Nobody else could have him this way. His attention would always be hers.

What would she want from him tonight? Madeline licked her lips as idea after idea filled her head. She wanted something depraved. She wanted him to show her how much he enjoyed her affection. How far he was willing to go to bring her pleasure.

Use the electro pads, Tan, she typed into the chat and watched as his moonlight-grey eyes darkened as he read her message. He breathed out heavily, groaning on the exhale.

"You're so fucking hot, Bookworm. As you wish," he whispered and sat up from his armchair, allowing her a spectacular view of his toned arse cheeks as he did so.

The compulsion to bite them was extreme and she had to hold in a moan at the sight.

Madeline pulled herself underneath her bedsheets, slid her panties to one side and grabbed her dildo from her bedside table. She had bought it on an impulse a few weeks ago when she noticed it was close in size and shape to Tan's. The only thing missing was his array of piercings that she was desperate to feel against her swollen clit.

"Where do you want them?" He asked, pulling his miniature mic to his lips beneath the mask so that his graveled voice felt as though he was right beside her, whispering in her ear.

Fuck, he didn't even need to try that hard.

One on each of your pecs. The other two on your inner thighs.

She typed her message quickly, aching to see his body tense with the shocks those pads would give him. If only she could control them herself. She would give anything to hold that little remote control and shock him by her own hand. It would be better that way, more intense, as he wouldn't know when it would come. He'd have to wait, on edge, in anticipation to feel that shock to his system.

If she could only suck his cock at the same time, her life would feel practically complete.

When he tutted his tongue on the roof of his mouth, slowly and seductively, her brows furrowed and a whine escaped her throat. He wouldn't deny her, would he? Not when she was so close to witnessing something so spectacular.

"You might have power over me, baby, but manners cost nothing."

Immediately, without even thinking, she typed, *Please. Fucking please!*

"That's much better. As you command. To everybody else watching and to all of my new followers, thank you for the support. If you've not watched my shock shows before, you're in for a treat."

Madeline could tell he finished his sentence on a smirk by the way his eyes crinkled at the corners. The smug git was so cock-sure, with no doubt as to why when he paraded around with the monster between his thighs, and he wore it well. He knew what his confidence did to his viewers. He got off, literally, on the reactions they gave him, the messages he received and the gifts he was given.

Some viewers had even proposed marriage to him during his stream in the past, much to Madeline's annoyance. She would never have the guts but the sentiment was there.

She only had the little issue of remembering who he was during the daytime.

"Ah, fuck!" He yelled as the first blast of electricity struck the pads on his inner thighs. His stiffened cock bobbed with pleasure and his chest rose and fell rapidly with his hard pants of breath.

He was fucking *Godly*.

Madeline teased her dildo up and down her wettened folds and circled the tip around the bud of her clit, imagining it was him.

"Mm, that stings so good," he groaned.

She pushed the large head of her toy inside herself and began to twist her wrist with a few languid strokes.

"I hope—" Tan breathed out before his eyes squeezed shut with the shock of pain providing him such delicious ecstasy. "I hope you're fucking happy with yourself, Bookworm."

Very, she replied. *I love when I make you scream.*

Tan bent forward towards his screen to be able to read her message and, when he looked back to the camera, he looked positively feral.

"Are you using my cock, baby?"

Madeline might have let slip that she used a dildo to fuck herself with, imagining it was him, during a stream last week when she'd had a little too much to drink. It was an accident really. Or perhaps, more likely, it wasn't. A part of her wanted Tan to know that she thought of him. That she *wanted* him. That her waking and sleeping thoughts were consumed by him.

Even when she was physically in Atlas Bentley's presence, she fantasised about Tan and he knew it. He must have stood in meetings knowing that Bookworm97 would be thinking about him, wherever she was in the world, and that's the way it would stay. For Madeline, her privacy was absolute and she would die of humiliation were he to ever find out who she was. That the woman who sat, begrudgingly, one desk down from him in the office was his biggest admirer. He would only use the knowledge to his advantage and she dreaded to think just how he would do so.

Swarms of messages from other viewers filled the chat:

Give me your cock, handsome.

Fuck me, please.

TIP! £40 - All for you.

But it was her message he was waiting for, she knew. His unwavering stare remained on the camera lens, daring her to answer him while his hand moved in long strokes up and down his length. The tip of his cock began to leak and Madeline licked her lips.

How could she refuse him?

Of course. Your cock feels so good inside my pussy.

Tan squeezed his red, swollen head as he read her message and she was sure that she would die for the chance to soothe it with her tongue.

"Such a little whore," he grumbled and his eyes crinkled at the corners once again.

"Oh fuck," she whispered to herself and pumped his cock into her dripping cunt harder, banging it against that fleshy part deep inside that she wished he would discover for himself. He had never called her anything other than 'Baby' or 'Bookworm' before so to think that she had now progressed to being his whore was something that made her eyes roll backwards in her head as her orgasm built and built.

With another intense shock to his pecs, making them flinch in response, his cock pulsed shooting thick, hot ropes of cum up his chest, splattering upon the corner of his mask and dripping down his abdomen.

"Atlas!" She moaned as she came, falling over the edge into an orgasm that made her vision double. Madeline immediately clasped her hand over her mouth as she rode out the waves of her high, her eyes wide with shock as she realised what she had done.

As her mind spun with every possible reason that she might have betrayed herself, screaming her rival's name instead of his sexy counterpart, she didn't even take notice of him wrapping up his show for the evening until she heard him call out her username.

"...for everybody who watched tonight. Your comments and tips are so, so appreciated and get ready for more fun, same time tomorrow. Bookworm97, baby, this show was for you and because you're such a big supporter, I want to give you a private show. Stick around and let me treat you."

Her heart thudded in her chest, hard enough to crack a rib or two, while she considered how to answer but, realistically, her mind was already made up. How could she possibly argue with a request like that?

It was tempting to do as he said, even after her mixup at the point of her orgasm - she would have to reprimand herself later for getting it so wrong - as he had never given her a private show before. She was intrigued, to say the least, and could definitely go again if he could. She knew he could. Madeline had never before witnessed a man with the same level of stamina as Tan and his ability to go for a few rounds was something she had marvelled at.

Most men she'd been with would be good for long enough to make themselves cum and then they'd ignore her, roll over and fall asleep.

Tan, however, was an animal and wasn't satisfied until his viewers were left sated and exhausted. Until they trickled off the stream one-by-one until only the most intensive watchers remained. For that reason, she was shocked that he would cut off his livestream so early just to dedicate time to her. But the thrill that shot through her body convinced her to stick around, curious as to what he was going to say.

I'll stay, Tan. For you, she typed.

His lips shuffled underneath his mask and she wondered what he was doing. Sticking out his tongue? Lord have mercy on her. Biting his lip? She needed more. That was the other benefit of the mask; it made everything feel so much more intense. She was constantly wondering what he was thinking and how he was reacting to the pleasure, to his viewers' messages too, when all she could see of him was his eyes.

Madeline watched as the viewer count on his stream ticked down to one. Only her and him. Alone at last.

"Did you like the show?" He drawled and began to peel the electro-pads from his chest and thighs. Madeline's eyes followed the movement, studying the travel of his fingers, the dexterity with which he used them.

Atlas Bentley's hands, she had to admit, were the sexiest part of him too. She had taken notice of them in board meetings when he would rub a thumb over his bottom lip while deep in thought. She'd admired the length and thickness of his fingers when they'd wrapped around a pen as he took notes. At the time, she had pushed down all thoughts like that. Repressed them back into the recesses of her mind where they belonged. Now, as she looked upon Tan's hands, it became difficult to separate the two.

I loved it. Let me show you how much.

As practised as the action was, she quickly clicked on the button to leave a tip and hoped he would appreciate her gift.

TIP! £500.

His eyes widened in surprise and his jaw dropped. She hid the smile he gave her behind the palm of her hand as though he could see her. She was glad he couldn't or else he might have also noticed the blush on her cheeks. Madeline had a knack for becoming giddy around this man with minimal effort on his part.

"You—" he laughed out breathily, *dreamily*, and it made her want to tip him that much again. "You didn't have to do that but you always look after me, don't you, baby?"

Always, she replied.

His eyes darkened once more and he began to touch his now hardening cock, playing with the piercings at his slit. She wondered if they provided any more pleasure or sensitivity. She wanted to find out first hand.

"Did you come?"

Madeline nodded to herself like an idiot before remembering that she had to type out her response.

Yes.

"How many times?"

Just once.

His eyebrows pinched together sharply as though she'd pissed him off with her response.

"Just once?" He lifted up his mask to reveal his lips and she thought of kissing them then for the first time. It was odd really that she had never thought so before, she supposed if she had it would put her in dangerous territory of wanting more than just Tan. Of wanting Atlas Bentley too. And that just wasn't acceptable.

He ran his tongue flatly across his palm, getting it wet, and wrapped it around his cock again. Her eyes dipped there immediately.

"That's not fucking good enough, baby."

I'm sorry.

"Don't be sorry. I just need to be better for you then, don't I?"

Tan grunted and pulled his bottom lip between his teeth as he brought his other hand down to cup his balls, squeezing them gently.

You're perfect as you are.

"Shut up," he snapped out of nowhere. Did she say something wrong?

"Get that dildo and fuck yourself. *Hard.* I don't want you thinking about anything but me sliding into that slick pussy of yours."

Fuck, his naughty mouth could get him in trouble and she would be riding the train to hell right alongside him. Madeline did as she was told and began to pound her silicone cock into her cunt, wishing he was there to lick her clean when she came.

I feel so full of you, Tan.

"Fuck. When are you going to admit that you want me?" He asked and she was momentarily ripped out of her fantasy whilst he continued to fuck himself with his hand. She could see how tight he was gripping himself by the tone of his knuckles. All colour had drained away from them and his face strained with the need to cum.

What did he mean? Had she not shown enough that she wanted him? Was being his highest tipper not appreciative enough for him?

I want you so badly.

"How long is it going to fucking take?" He growled, the sound shooting to her clit and it was nearly enough to topple her over the edge but something was holding her back. The fact that she had no clue what he was talking about anymore.

She imagined he was asking how long it would take for her to cum so that he could follow her into bliss but, judging by the tension in his jaw, she knew it was something else. Something she didn't know about.

She remained silent, waiting for him to just spit out whatever it was he meant. Whatever it was that he clearly *needed* to say. Her orgasm was so, so close and by the looks of his twitching cock, so was his.

"You don't think I'm clever enough to work it out? You don't think I worked it out ages ago? Do you know how fucking hard it has been to watch you pine after me and hate me at the same time?"

Madeline shuffled up her bed, pulling the dildo out of her desperate pussy and her knees to her chest, as she realised what he was saying. He'd found her. Figured it out.

FUCK.

How he'd done it, she wasn't sure, but if he meant what he said, then Atlas Bentley had been going along with her little indiscretion for a while. Her heart thudded, her head span and her cheeks flushed as he tore off the mask entirely, baring that familiar, stupidly attractive face to the camera.

"Oh come on, baby," he teased, noticing her silence. "I was bound to work it out eventually. Did you really think Bookworm97 was the most top-secret username? I know when you were born, I know more about you than you think I do. Do you really believe that I haven't noticed your adorable little blush every time you bump into me at work? Every time I catch you looking over at my desk?"

I do nothing of the sort.

He laughed. That breathy sort-of turned on laugh that Tan would use to bring her off. Now, however, it was Atlas Bentley who was using that laugh. Confusing her, leaving conflicted thoughts to wind and twist within her mind, tormenting her, torturing her.

"You do, sweet girl." He hesitated for a moment as though in thought. "You've stopped fucking yourself, haven't you? I didn't tell you to stop. Put my cock back inside that needy little cunt until it's dripping wet. You're going to cum for me one more time."

Madeline whimpered in response, her clit throbbing, her core aching for release. His words were so filthy and just what she had always wanted to hear from Tan. Exactly what she'd always needed for him to say to her. Except that it wasn't Tan speaking to her now. It was a thoroughly turned on Atlas Bentley who had continued stroking his cock with the passion that her online crush always had.

If he had known her identity all this time, why was he still touching himself? She had always thought that if he ever figured out who she was, he would be disgusted and would humiliate her in front of the whole office. But... he looked as though he wanted this just as much as she did and she believed him. Believed that he wanted her pleasure for his own.

So she tried to push down her hatred for the sake of releasing the tension that had crawled up her spine at having edged herself so close just to be disappointed. Madeline grabbed her dildo, sucked it into her mouth for a moment while she watched him staring down the camera, and pushed it back into her willing pussy.

Okay, is all she said in response but his answering smirk was all she needed.

"That's a good fucking girl. I'm so close, baby, you know how to get me *so* fucking ready."

Madeline's bedroom was filled with breathy pants, little whines of pleasure, and the sound of Atlas— Tan— *whoever* he was - wanking his cock and groaning through her laptop speakers.

"Admit that you want me," he commanded.

No.

He snarled, his lip curling upwards, "What will it take?"

She thought about it for a moment. What would make it possible for them to carry on, for *her* to continue for long enough to finish? To admit that she wanted this man who wore the face of her rival during the day and her obsession at night.

Put the mask back on.

He grinned beautifully. Atlas truly was a stunning man. Sexy, gorgeous, everything she would dream about her perfect man looking like. It was just such a shame his attitude and behaviour didn't match that vision and she couldn't align herself between the two. Without that stupid mask, Madeline couldn't alter her mindset from hating him whilst he was attempting to set her skin on fire using his own.

Whatever the reason was behind her ability to separate them as soon as that mask was tied around his head, she needed it. She refused to lose Tan when he was the only man that made her feel this way.

It was selfish but she didn't care.

"So..." His voice strained as he tightened his skull and crossbones mask behind his head. "If I keep this mask on..."

Tan adjusted his camera to zoom in closer so that she could watch his cock leak pre-cum in high definition. Her eyelashes fluttered, her core clamped down around Tan's replacement cock and she gripped her bedsheets in her fist as her high approached.

"And tell you my address..."

Her eyes widened as she listened to his throaty voice, deep and alluring, coaxing her closer and closer. His cock looked about ready to burst.

"Will you come?"

Madeline sucked in a gasp and brought her hand to her clit, rubbing furiously at the swollen bud, while she fucked herself with the other.

"Will you come for me, baby?"

She lifted her hand to her mouth and bit down against it as she came for him all over the dildo, leaving a wet patch on the bed as her juices coated her arsecheeks and thighs.

I'll do anything you ask, she wrote after scrambling to type once she'd recovered from the aftershocks racing through her body. She *would* do anything for him too, she wasn't lying. She'd fantasised for months about Tan inviting her over to his apartment for more and now he had. She wasn't exactly going to turn him down but there was one condition.

As long as you keep the mask on.

Reading her message was enough for him to follow her into a voice-breaking orgasm. His groan was loud and powerful and made her ready to go again instantaneously. His cum coated his toned body, sliding down his hunched frame and ruining the soft fabric of the armchair he was sitting on. It was the second load he'd deposited upon himself that evening and her mouth became wetter at the thought of licking it off him.

"Anything you want, Bookworm," he panted. "My address is 127 Cedarwood Drive. I'll expect you within thirty minutes. The door is open. Come and clean me up. Tongue only." His eyes crinkled and she bit her lip. "Then I'll fuck your sweet cunt just as you want me to."

I'll be there.

Tan laughed devilishly, "You have no idea how long I've waited to show my biggest supporter my appreciation."

Chapter 3 - 127 Cedarwood Drive

When Madeline arrived, apprehensively, at 127 Cedarwood Drive, she took a moment to look upwards and take in the breathtaking building before her. It was an old Victorian three-story townhouse in the center of London. The thing even looked like it had a loft conversion meaning the rent must be expensive as fuck.

Though Atlas Bentley was rich beyond all belief so that fact would hardly matter to him. An heir to a fortune, the descendent of Lords and Barons and who knows what else stretching back hundreds of years. His father was one of the Councilmen for a neighbouring district and it seemed that the apple didn't fall far from the tree. Atlas was going to be next in line to hold that political title within the family. Over her dead body was it going to be within Madeline's district however. She knew this place, grew up amongst the people and listened to what they needed.

He just wanted the glory that the title came with, she suspected. He didn't care about the responsibility associated with it. It was why she had fought and worked her hands to the bone for the last year on her campaign to beat him to the post and was still waiting to hear if she'd been successful after his last attempt at sabotage nearly ruined everything.

He drove her up the wall, to put it mildly, and she hated him. Truly she did but it didn't stop her from wanting to fuck him until he passed out or she did. Whichever came first. As long as he kept the mask on.

She slowly walked up the steps to his front door and twisted the ornate gold doorknob, testing to see if he had in fact left it open for her. Madeline was pleased to find that he had and pushed the door open. It made a loud but satisfying click as she closed it and she knew that, wherever he was in this massive place, that he would have heard it.

Taking off her coat, which had protected her from the soft drizzle of rain, and her shoes in the hallway, she took a look around. There were framed paintings all over the walls - some Picasso, some Van Gogh, some Georgia O'Keefe - and they all looked like original works. Her jaw dropped in shock the further she walked through his house as she entered his lounge which contained large leather couches, a chandelier dripping from the ceiling and a wall-to-wall bookshelf.

She wanted to curl up and die right there with a book in her hand. If the paintings were original, she could only imagine the type of books he owned but that wasn't what she was there for.

As he'd instructed her, she was there to lick him clean and then get fucked. Wouldn't Dahlia be proud if she could see her now?

Madeline continued exploring his property as she climbed the elegant staircase to the upper floor, where she imagined his bedroom might be. She didn't have a clue which room he'd use to stream from but could only imagine that a person wouldn't perform the types of acts that he had on the ground floor. Peeping neighbours and all that.

On the final step up to the first floor, the wooden boards beneath her feet creaked and she sucked in a gasp. She didn't really know why. It wasn't as though he didn't know she was there. Though there was something about tiptoeing through his house, like he was a predator and she was his prey, that turned her on.

Would he jump out and pull her down underneath him? Would he wait for her to approach him? She didn't know and it was building up her excitement.

She pushed open several large mahogany doors trying to find him but came up empty. The second floor showed no sign of him either and that's when she remembered that, from the outside, the loft light had been on.

LATE NIGHTS

Madeline climbed the last set of stairs slowly, looking up at the closed door she knew he was hiding behind, as she imagined what might happen to her that evening. She had told him that he could do anything with her he wanted so long as he respected her rule and that left a lot of room for opportunity.

Pushing open the door to the loft, her jaw dropped at the sight of him sitting in the green velvet armchair he always used for his streams. The light in the room was dimmed, casting delicious shadows over his skin, illuminating his toned chest and thighs. It bounced off his messy blond hair perfectly, giving him an illusion of a halo upon his head. She could have laughed at the irony were she not trembling by the door.

Thankfully, he had listened to her request and his mask was tied securely where it belonged so that she could enjoy the man she'd been obsessing over for half a year.

"Took you long enough," he drawled, not bothering to stand up.

Tan laid his hands on each of the armrests as he took in her body from head to toe. Madeline had been wearing nothing but her pyjamas during his stream so had scrambled to find something in her wardrobe that he might like. In the end, she went for a tight red slip dress that accented her breasts. His flaccid cock laid on his thigh but twitched awake at the sight of her. She smiled shyly before answering him.

"You gave me thirty minutes. It's been twenty-one."

When she looked at him a little closer, she could see the streaks of cum that had dripped down his body and her mouth began to salivate as she considered the task he had given her.

Tan's eyes darkened and she suddenly felt like she needed to pay attention.

"Let's get one thing straight. On the stream, I do what *you* want. You're the customer, you get what you ask for but here..." his silver eyes crinkled at the corners as he smirked beneath his mask. "Here, you're mine. You don't answer me back. You don't misbehave and you do everything I tell you to. Do you understand..." he paused as he considered what to call her. "*Bookworm?*"

She gulped and nodded her head, lowering herself to her knees to let him know that she was ready to be submissive. That he was her master for the night and she'd let him take what he wanted.

"That's it. Crawl to me, baby."

Madeline did as she was told and slowly approached him on her hands and knees. She briefly looked up and to the left to see his camera and lighting set up. His laptop was settled on a desk just to the side of his chair. How weird it was that she was now behind the scenes.

When she reached his feet, she looked up at him to ask for her next instruction.

"Stick out your tongue," he commanded in that deep voice that sent a shiver through her body. "Good girl, now you're going to start here and you're not going to leave a drop."

He pointed to his right pectoral where she could see a trail of cum glistening under the spotlight. Madeline set to work and, as with everything she had ever put her mind to, she committed her entire energy to the job. She licked every single bead of come that had settled upon his alabaster skin and savoured the taste each time she did so, playing with it on her tongue, letting it dribble down her chin. He tasted like heaven and sin all at the same time and she knew, if she had any more of him, that she wouldn't want to taste anything else for as long as she lived.

And she had waited for this opportunity to taste him for far too long. It was her turn to put on a show now.

Losing his patience however, Tan— yes, Tan, he was definitely still Tan— leaned forward and squeezed her cheeks together firmly. The come that coated her tongue slowly fell off her tongue as he did so and he watched it drip to the floor.

"Wasteful." He tutted, forcing her to look at the mess she had made. "You like being fed, huh?"

She nodded her head as much as she could whilst he was holding her so tightly. His cock was now hard again and bobbed against his stomach every time she dipped her eyes to look at it. He gripped himself at the base and brought it closer to her so that she might see his piercings in better detail.

She studied every silver hoop and stud that decorated his thick length and stuck her tongue out again, hoping he would take the hint and push it inside her waiting mouth.

He merely laughed and dropped his hand from her face, leaving her wondering if she'd done something wrong.

"Do you know what red, yellow and green mean, Harp—" her heart thumped and blood raced as he almost slipped up. Almost ruined the moment. Almost destroyed her beautiful illusion. "Baby?"

Madeline hadn't experimented much with the principles of domination and submission before but she'd read about the subject. Only after Tan had mentioned on a stream once that he enjoyed it. So when she thought about his question, all she could do in answer was to nod her head.

"I want to hear it. Explain them for me."

She went to speak but her voice came out rather muffled, her throat still coated with his come. She swallowed hard and began again.

"Green means that I'm happy with what we're doing. Yellow means to slow down and ease up. Red means to stop immediately."

"Mmm, you have done your research, haven't you? Good. So when I do this..."

He placed both hands into her nest of wild curls and dragged her up into a standing position from the floor. She let out a little whimper as the pain in her scalp traveled straight to her clit.

"…what colour are you?"

"Green," she breathed out as he pulled her face closer to his. His mask tickled her jaw.

"Good. Now get back down on your knees, whore, you're going to help me gain some more followers."

He walked over to his camera, turning it on, and typed a message on his social media channels to inform his subscribers that he would be going live again in a few minutes. Taking a seat back in his armchair, he pulled her closer to settle between his strong thighs.

"What…? What are we doing?" She asked nervously.

"You're going to suck my cock and swallow me down whilst my fans watch."

Fuck. Okay.

She waited as the seconds ticked down to his stream turning live with her hands clasping onto each other behind her back.

"Stick out your arse. I want something to look at while you take this," he told her and gave his cock a quick pump right before her eyes. She reshuffled herself to fulfil his request and the skirt of her dress rode up a little, baring the tanned olive skin of her arse to him.

His eyes were too busy taking her in to notice the blinking red light, signifying that his stream was live, for a few moments before she leaned down to lightly bite his thigh, letting him know.

"Ow, you little—" he jumped, forcing his eyes to face forward as he cupped her jaw and she fought to hide a smile.

"Hey guys! I've got a special treat for us all tonight. So special that I just had to resume my stream and share with you. You remember Bookworm? My highest tipper? Well she's found a way to sneak into my house. And now I'm going to punish her slutty little throat. Bookworm..." he addressed her then directly. "...since you won't be able to speak, tap twice on my thigh for yellow and once hard for red, okay?"

She nodded, her riotous curls bouncing down her back in full view of the camera. She was ready but she thought that he would enter her mouth slowly.

How wrong she had been.

Standing, he gripped each side of her face and used her mouth like his fleshlight, fucking it hard and deep. All she could do was hold onto his thighs as he thrust himself against her tongue, hitting the back of her throat.

He groaned, "Fuck, such a good little whore. You guys jealous yet?"

Madeline watched from the corner of her eye as he bent forwards slightly, pushing himself further into her mouth, as he read the incoming messages.

I wish I was Bookworm.

Why don't I ever get an invite?

Fuck her, Tan. Use her fucking throat.

The piercings at the tip of his cock were cold against the walls of her throat and her eyes rolled backwards at the sensation while she took her punishment. The thrust of his hips was so powerful that she could only imagine how good it would feel to have him ruin her pussy. She could feel herself dripping down her thighs, having forgone any panties for him to have easy access, while he fucked her throat as though he wouldn't get another opportunity.

It was a good job that she had practiced sucking off her dildo, that measured the same thickness and length as him, to enable her to take him so well without gagging. Such a good idea as it was, she hadn't ever expected to have his actual cock in her mouth. But she had hoped and imagined. Oh boy, had she imagined it. But as good as her imagination was, the real thing blew her mind.

Madeline sucked his cock harder when she felt it starting to pulse against her tongue. His breathing had become erratic and she knew he was close. She'd take it all too. Would take anything he was willing to give. After all, she had been fantasising over this man for six months, had only dreamed that she would be in the position she was between his thighs and wished, only for a brief second, that he would take off the mask so that she could see his reactions.

But no, that was dangerous thinking. She didn't know how she would react if he did so and she worried that it would put her off. Make her want to leave.

With only a second's warning when his eyes shone with lust, he spilled load after load of come into her mouth and thrust inside a few more times to make sure she didn't waste a drop.

"Show me," he panted, dragging himself out and allowing her a moment to catch her breath. She stuck her tongue out to show that she had taken all of him down her throat just as he wanted then wiped the tears from her cheeks when he was satisfied.

He growled, proud of her for taking him so well, and sat back in his chair while he regained his breath. She didn't know how but he'd had three orgasms now tonight. Tan was a machine, so good at this. At showing his viewers what they wanted. She loved it. But he must have been exhausted.

"I've got to go," he growled into his mic that was expertly positioned upon the hem of his mask. "This whore is begging to be fucked with an ass like that." Her eyes widened in surprise to hear him talk about her this way. Her core ached for him, despite the fact that she'd come twice already. She didn't care. She just needed him. "See you all tomorrow," he signed off abruptly with a wink to the camera and Madeline noticed that messages were still rapidly pinging through on his laptop when he closed the lid.

Scooping her up off the floor and wrapping her legs around his waist, he walked them over to the plush four-poster bed that she hadn't yet spotted in the corner of the room. He didn't really ever use it, preferring his armchair set up instead. He slammed her body down onto the mattress and leaned over her to suck red sores into her neck that would last for days.

"You drive me fucking crazy."

Did she? That was news to Madeline but made sense as to why he continued touching himself during their private show. It was hard to come to terms with the fact that he was attracted to her or maybe he was just taking advantage of how turned on he had made her during the show. Benefiting from her obvious infatuation with his masked persona.

"Ditto," she moaned and she dug her nails into his scalp, feeling his soft blond hair between her fingers. Finally.

"You make me want to do stupid things..."

What was he talking about? She wanted him to do less talking and just fucking take her already. Had she not waited long enough?

"Like what?" She gasped as he sucked her earlobe into his mouth.

"Do you like this dress?"

"What?"

"Do you like it, Harper?"

The use of her real name eluded her in her lust-filled haze. She was hardly conscious enough as the pleasure of his touch distracted her beyond all comprehension to take notice.

"It's okay," she answered when she pieced together what he was asking. "I chose it because I thought you might like it."

"I fucking love it," he grumbled. "But it has got to go."

Taking her by surprise, he tore the red dress directly down the middle, baring her breasts and slick cunt to him. Underwear was overrated, she didn't need it, but oh if only she could have seen him bite his lip as he stared down at her body. She would have quite liked to watch his face turn desperate for her upon seeing her naked for the first time.

She was well-rounded, she knew, even for a short girl. Her breasts were large but perky and she had a tight stomach from her regular swimming workouts. His eyes dazzled under the spotlights in his loft as he pulled back from her, leaving her alone on his silk sheets, to take her in fully.

Atlas— Tan— what was she supposed to call him again?— ran a hand down his face, over the mask, before it settled over his covered mouth. He exhaled harshly.

"I'm going to fucking devour you," he growled and she spread her thighs in response, showing him how wet sucking his cock had made her.

"Please do," she whimpered.

No time was wasted before he gripped his large hands underneath her arse, pulling her towards the end of the bed and her eyes shot wide as she leaned up on her elbows, preparing to watch him lower to his knees. He pushed her thighs backwards and slid a slow finger between her folds, pumping once. His delirious eyes fixed to her face, watching for every quirk, every bite to her lower lip and every moan that would escape her sore throat.

When Tan began to pull up his mask, a pang of panic shot up her spine and her breath came out in heavy pants but she was quickly soothed when his lips squeezed together around her clit. He kissed her there at first, feeling her softness against his lips, before he delved his tongue between her folds. The feeling was like no other and she refused to drag her eyes away from his.

She would let him taste her and eat her up all night if he wanted to and she got the impression that he did by the way he would groan against her sensitive bud. When he pushed another thick finger into her pussy, she clenched around them as the knot behind her navel began to build. Madeline was desperate for release despite how many times she had come already that night.

He just inspired the best out of her.

"That's it, baby. I can feel you clenching my fingers. Fuck, I'm not going to be able to last long inside you," he brought his hand down from her thigh to squeeze the base of his once-again hardened cock.

"You— You can— g-go again?" She stuttered as he built her closer and closer.

"Even if I couldn't, I would find a way to get hard for this perfect pussy. You're not leaving here until I've had you, you little whore. I deserve it. Now shut up and come for me."

Madeline didn't know what he meant when he said he deserved to have her. But, regardless, she could do nothing but agree when disagreeing might make him stop. So she did as she was bid like the good girl he'd taught her to be and came all over his tongue and fingers.

The sounds he made as he licked her clean were so delicious. His tongue laid flat against the crease of her upper thigh, running along her sticky folds, and that was the first time she'd seen him squeeze his eyes shut tight for a few moments while he concentrated on tasting her.

"So fucking sweet," he said as he smacked his lips together, having finished lapping up her juices from his chin. "Oh, you needed that, didn't you Harper? It's been a while, hasn't it?"

She nodded, her own eyes shut now as she swam in her own head, drained from coming for him a third time within a few hours. His deep register lulled her into a net of safety and his sheets were so, so soft.

"Hey," he snapped his fingers. "None of that."

He came to straddle her chest, pinning her arms to her side, his hard cock bouncing before her face. Tan's lookalike laid his palm across her cheek, patting it softly in an attempt to rouse her into consciousness.

"Stay awake. I'm not done with you yet. You can give me one more, baby. I need to feel this cunt fluttering around my cock. Just once."

It was almost a promise and because she felt safe around him, strange as the thought was at the time, she nodded her head and brought herself to her knees once he'd moved off her. He eyed her and consciously pulled his mask back down his face.

She really wanted to kiss him, his full lips were drawing her in, but it was forbidden. Madeline had forbidden it herself but now, she was struggling to remember why.

Her eyes fell to his red and swollen cock and she wished he would just push it into her and show her Heaven.

"Will you ever kiss me?" He asked then as though reading her mind.

She shook her head from side to side, "No. I-I can't."

"And why the hell not?"

His brow was pinched. He wasn't happy with her response. He wanted to kiss her.

"You're a bully."

His face was still beneath the mask, giving nothing away.

"Would you kiss your Tan?" He mocked.

"Yes! You're not him. Not right now. You're— you're acting like—"

"Like Atlas? Hate to break it to you but we're one and the same."

"No," she shook her head again and gripped her thighs in her anger. His gaze fell there immediately. "You're different. He's perfect and mine. Atlas is cruel and goes out of his way to show me he hates me."

"Atlas doesn't hate you, baby," he said in that soft voice again. The soothing one. The one that belonged to Tan and her heart melted and her skin heated. It always did when he was around.

"I don't want to talk about him."

"Then let me fuck the thought out of you."

Securely assured that the man she was about to have sex with was the man of her dreams once again, she let him spread her wide and use his cock, the little silver balls on the tip of it, to massage her clit. The cool steel felt exquisite and she keened under his touch.

"I've thought about this a lot. For a long time," he moaned as he pushed his thick head through her wet folds.

He was big. She knew he was. Had even stretched herself out to his size but the only thing her dildo couldn't do was get harder with arousal. He was practically rock solid as he entered her and it felt so good.

"Such a good girl, take a little more."

Tan inched himself inside of her a little bit more at a time. Both of them were lost for breath, struggling to fill their lungs as their eyes met.

"I want it all," she bit her lip, pleading her case.

"And you'll have it. My highest tipper gets the best. Nobody else gets this treatment. Only you," he assured her and she smiled widely up at him. "So fucking beautiful."

His thumb came to brush against her bottom lip. The movement was so tender, so warm that she thought her little obsession could very easily have progressed into something more. Something scary and heart-wrenching and unfamiliar.

"Fuck me... Please."

"As you command, baby," and his cock filled her up to the hilt.

For support, he wrapped his tattoo covered hands around her neck as he dragged himself out of her to the tip before thrusting back inside her welcoming cunt. Over and over and over again until she became almost incomprehensible.

"T-T-Tan," she moaned into his neck, clinging onto his back by her nails and causing spots of blood to quicken to the surface of his alabaster skin.

"Kiss me, Bookworm. Please," his voice was strained and she couldn't refuse him. Not Tan. Not when he asked so nicely.

She pulled him closer, her arms around his neck, as she placed an open-mouth kiss against his covered lips. Madeline felt him kiss her back through the mask, his brows pinched and eyes squeezed shut while he continued his relentless assault to her dripping pussy.

"Colour?" He asked through panted breaths.

"Green. Green. Green."

It was fantastic. Perfect. Everything she thought it would be. Enough to throw her over the edge into yet another orgasm.

But then he went and ruined it. He ripped off his mask entirely so that she was staring up at the face of Atlas Bentley.

"What about now?"

"I—I—" she stammered in shock.

Madeline didn't know how she felt. It was all too much. His pounding hips, rippling muscles, smooth skin and seductive voice were all emphatic pros of this situation. Atlas' biting tone and revealed face reminded her of everything he had done to her. To hurt her. To ruin her.

But it didn't matter. She wanted the man currently filling her up more than she had ever desired anything in her life. Even if he was her biggest rival. She would deal with that another time.

"What colour are you now, baby?" He asked, not letting up for a moment in his movements.

"Green," she cried and gripped the bedsheets beneath her. Tears sprung to her eyes.

"Green? You're sure?"

She nodded.

"Then why—"

"I hate you!"

"No, you don't. You can't. We're the same, Harper."

"I do," she nodded again. "I hate you."

The expression on Atlas' face then confused her. It was a mix of anger, irritation and hurt. And when he looked so much like the man she had slowly and deeply fallen for, she realised it hurt her too.

"Then fuck me like you hate me," he growled and pulled her on top of him, straddling his waist.

"Oh, fuck," she screamed and began to roll her hips, taking his cock deeper than before. He pushed against her inner walls so fucking spectacularly and she just knew that his piercings would feel good. They worked to stimulate her g-spot like no toy she'd ever tried did. He was perfection and more tears rolled down her cheeks as she thought that she would have to give him up when reality hit.

Madeline's little hands pressed down on the sides of his throat, just as he had done to her, and the power she held felt incredible. She could do it. She could hurt him, if she wanted. She could use his OnlyFans account to ruin him. Run to the Councilman with it. Push him out of the running and fix her career. She would win.

But she couldn't.

No part of her could bring herself to lose him. Tan, Atlas, neither of them, as their faces began to merge.

"That's it, baby. See? It's me," he breathed, blurring the lines of the man she despised and the man she loved.

Madeline removed her hands from his neck, noting the red lines she'd created there, and placed them on either side of his handsome face instead as she crushed her lips to his.

His kiss was heady and pure and filled with a long-overdue sense of desire from both sides. It was as though she had always known his lips would be soft and warm, passionate and giving just like him. The Atlas she used to know would never have kissed her like this, like his world would fall apart if she pulled away, and Tan, in all of his sexual wisdom, would never have the care for her to tease every moan from her lips.

But together, finally recognised as one, she felt overwhelming relief.

As their tongues tangled together, it was all they needed to fall over the edge into one blissful and final orgasm. Atlas filled her up with his seed just as she'd always wanted and he pulled her into his chest tightly, wrapping his arms around her back, to prevent her from leaving as he feared she would.

"Don't go," he whispered into her ear, taking a deep inhale against her curls.

"I couldn't even if I wanted to," she joked, kissing him again, and ripping a tired but heavenly laugh from his lips.

Chapter 4 - Stupid Things

The next morning, Madeline sat opposite Councilman Gilbert's desk, tired and aching like hell, waiting for him to give her the news. Good or bad, fucking elating or heartbreaking. She just needed to know if her hard work had paid off. If she'd achieved her dream or not. If she hadn't, she could try again. If she had, she didn't know what she would do first but suspected that a celebration would be in order.

Either way though, she couldn't have what she really wanted. She couldn't have Atlas.

If she won, it would mean he had lost and he might hate her back in that eventuality. Never to speak to her again. If she had lost, she knew she wouldn't be able to even look at him as his efforts to thwart her campaign would have been successful. She wouldn't be able to forgive him for that. Ever.

She was more nervous than she ever had been. More than when she started the job and more than when she'd arrived at Atlas' house yesterday, not knowing what could happen between them.

Everything rested on this. She had chewed her nails half to death that morning in anticipation.

Councilman Gilbert was a man in his forties with a shaved head and groomed, brunette beard. He scrubbed up well, to be sure, in his smart suits and expensive shoes. Madeline wondered, if she became Councilwoman, what outfits she would choose to wear to compete with him.

"Harper." He nodded to her in greeting as he entered his office. "I won't beat around the bush. There's been a development. It's frankly shocked me. I didn't see this coming." He sighed. "Bentley has pulled out the race."

Her jaw dropped. So that was why he hadn't turned up to the office that morning. She had woken up in his bed in the loft without him but assured herself that he perhaps had just gone to work early as she knew he sometimes did. A note would have been nice but she figured that she would see him shortly anyway. When he wasn't at work, however, her heart had begun to thud in her chest as she suspected something might have happened.

But... what? Why would he—?

"Something about it not feeling right and..." he sighed again, pushing his blazer out of the way to place his hands on his hips in clear disappointment. "I'll deal with that later but the good news is that you've done it."

He smiled and it took her a moment to register what he was saying.

"I've—?"

"You've won, Harper. Or should I call you *Councilwoman* Harper now?" He chuckled and she beamed, jumping up from her seat as though she was about to hug him before correcting herself and shaking his hand in thanks.

"The other candidates?" She wondered. There were plenty of other teams all aiming for this one spot.

"Weren't as popular as you. Well done, all that hard work was worth it, eh? I look forward to working with you, Harper. Now go, take the day to celebrate."

She shook his hand again, thanked him again too and exited his office, letting out a near silent scream when she reached the hallway. She didn't care if others watched her. In fact, many of them came to shake her hand in congrats, having assumed the news from her reaction.

"Oh! Harper, you should read this," Gilbert then interrupted and passed her a file.

"What is it, sir?"

"Those are the minutes from my meeting with Bentley. I think you would be interested to know his reasons."

With a lifted brow and upturned lips, Gilbert turned on his heel, sticking his hands in his pockets and walked back into his office without another word.

Madeline politely excused herself to her colleagues and ran straight down to one of the private meeting rooms where she would be able to sit and read in peace.

Present at time of meeting, 07:32am

Atlas Bentley, candidate for Camden Councilperson

Adrian Gilbert, current presiding Camden Councilman

AB - A moment of your time, Councilman?

AG - Of course, Atlas. Something bothering you?

AB - Yes, actually. I'm here to formally withdraw my campaign. I'm sorry to say that I entered the running under the wrong circumstances and I'm afraid that my situation has changed.

AG - Well, this is quite a surprise, Bentley. You and Harper were pretty much head to head for the position.

AB - She should get it.

AG - You don't have the ability to appoint her, unfortunately.

AB - I know that but hopefully my withdrawal and resignation will help her.

AG - Your resignation? You don't have to resign too, Bentley. There are other boroughs, other districts that you could run for. You're very good at what you do. What about your father? He'll be disappointed won't he?

AB - I don't care. Truth be told, I never cared. I only entered to appease him and well... I don't need to do that anymore.

AG - What are you going to do now then?

AB - Go after what I want.

AG - Well, I wish you the best of luck. I hope we get to work together in the future.

AB - Thank you, sir, but for the line of work I'll be entering into, I find it unlikely. Tell Harper I wish her congratulations. I have no doubt she'll win even after I tried to mess it all up for her.

AG - You're not going to tell her yourself?

AB - No, I'm leaving now. I just wanted to bow out gracefully, let her take the stage now. She's earned it.

AG - I'll let her know you send your best wishes.

AB - Thank you. Goodbye, sir.

Without even thinking, Madeline sprung to action. She clutched the file to her chest, not letting it go, and ran to her workspace. As she suspected, Atlas' desk had been cleared as though he was never there. Never had been and her heart ached at seeing it.

He couldn't just be gone. If he was, she would hunt him down. There was no way that she'd allow him to leave her like this. Without even a goodbye.

"Where's Bentley? Has anybody seen him this morning?" She asked, louder than possibly necessary so that everybody in the office could hear her.

Most people shrugged, having arrived to start their workday at 9am just as she had done. They'd all missed him.

But then—

"Er, Miss...? He left not long ago. Took his time packing his desk. Put something on yours I think."

Thank God for Gary, the regular office cleaner, who must have witnessed the whole thing that morning, having always taken the early shift.

She smiled to him in thanks and dashed across to her desk. There, amongst all of her clutter, sat an original copy of Charles Dickens' Great Expectations with a little sticky note placed upon the cover. Her fingers shook as she picked it up, so so carefully, and read his elegant handwriting.

For my bookworm,

This is what I have for you; Great Expectations. You'll go far, Harper, and even further now that I won't be there to ruin it all for you. I never wanted you to hate me, I hope you understand. It was never about that. If you're willing to hear me out then meet me at my place, the door will be open.

LATE NIGHTS

And don't even try to give me this back, it's yours.
Atlas

There was no question in her mind as to what she would do next. She ran outside, shouting a quick goodbye to her colleagues as she passed, and called a taxi to take her back to 127 Cedarwood Drive.

There, she stood by the front door for a moment, just as she had the night before, with apprehension swilling around her mind as she thought of every possibility once she pushed open that door. Would he tell her he never wanted her, that he did it all just for some fun and games? She desperately hoped not.

Pushing it open, she didn't bother to check any of the rooms as she passed like she had last time, suspecting where he would be. She barged through the door to his loft but found it empty, darkened and unused since last night. Madeline walked back down the stairs, not knowing where to begin.

Instead, having no patience to try to find him when she so desperately needed to talk to him, she yelled, "Atlas!"

"Fucking hell, Harper," his muffled voice came from one of the neighbouring rooms down the hall. He opened the door and stood with his arms crossed, leaning his back against the door jamb. He wore one of his usual work suits - a fitted slate grey that matched his eyes - but he'd loosened his top few buttons and tie, giving him a more casual look. It drove her mad. "Give a man a heart attack, why don't you?"

"I couldn't find you. Thought you'd be upstairs."

"No. I only go up there for my streams. I was just... lying in bed." He pointed into the room behind him, covering up a yawn with another hand, and she wanted desperately to go in. To see where he lays his head. To lie there with him too. He cleared his throat when she didn't speak, running a tattooed hand across the nape of his neck, "congratulations are in order, I hope?"

She nodded tearfully and he smiled widely, wider and more dazzling that she'd ever seen him.

"That's good," he nodded.

"Why did you do it?" She asked, unable to hold off for another second.

"Withdraw? I didn't want it as much as you did. I was pressured into running but I never saw myself as the Councilman. You deserved it."

"So then why—" she held herself together. "Why did you make my life hell? Why torment me and shoot down my hard work, embarrass me and my team in front of Gilbert?"

He looked at the floor for a second before rejoining their eye contact.

"I just... wanted you to notice me."

"Oh, I noticed you. I thought you were a conniving, ruinous little shit."

He laughed, nodding in agreement, and her heart melted but she continued.

"When I found your account, I was going to run straight to Gilbert or—or— I would have used it against you when you'd find a way to push my campaign back three steps more or—"

"Then why didn't you?" He interrupted, lowering his arms and taking a step towards her.

"Well, I—"

"You didn't do it for the same reason I irritated you in the first place."

"Which— which is?"

"I wanted your attention. That's right, isn't it? You didn't want to lose what you found in Tan? You wanted me to notice you through him? That's why you gave me so much fucking money. Too much, Harper."

She nodded.

"...but you would just sulk to yourself. I wanted you to get mad at me, to lash out, to say something," another step, "but you were just so stubborn, weren't you? You were just happy to hate me from a distance at work and fall apart for me at night. Why?"

Another step closer.

"I— I couldn't do it."

Closer.

"Why, baby? Admit it. Admit you wanted me, please. I need to hear it. I feel like I'm going out of my mind."

Even closer.

She sucked in a breath at the term of endearment. She couldn't refuse him. Not when he was finally saying everything she wanted him to, all of the right things. Not when Atlas was finally the man she could see herself being with.

"Yes, I liked you, okay?" She yelled, banging her fists against his chest when he stood only a foot away. "But I didn't like you too. You were perfect and horrible. You never said a nice word to me. Not even a 'good morning, how are you?' Nothing."

Atlas lifted his hand to the back of her neck, wrapping a few curls around his fingers.

"So you pretended?"

She nodded, "I could have what I wanted with Tan. He was nice to me, listened to me, gave me everything I wanted... Apart from you."

Madeline noticed Atlas' throat bob and his grip tightened slightly against the back of her neck when he pulled her closer. Her chest flushed against his as he wrapped his arms around her lower back.

That silvery gaze concentrated down at her, studying her face, and it was so nice to be able to look at him this closely, as she'd always liked to. He had soft freckles adorning his nose that were adorable and she had never seen them before, always being covered up during his stream. And she had refused to look at him properly out of sheer principle in the office.

"I'm sorry. I told you, didn't I? You make me do stupid things. Stupid, reckless, life changing things. Like resigning from the cleric's office."

She flattened her palms against his chest, running them down his torso a little and feeling the studs he'd had pushed through his nipples at her request. Her breath caught. She hadn't given them as much attention as she'd have liked last night. Wasn't able to show her appreciation fully in her delirious headspace, in the rush of it all. Perhaps— would he want to do all of that again?

"What are you going to do?" She asked, waiting to watch his face change, to watch his lips move, to study every detail about him that she had refused to notice before.

He laughed a little and pulled his lips to the side as if he was a little bashful. Atlas dropped his eyes from her, lowering his head and she wouldn't accept it. Not now. Not when she'd overcome so much to be able to look at him like this.

Madeline lifted her palm to his cheek, forcing him to turn back to her.

"I— I'm going to start my own business. I've been saving up money. Hoping to separate from my father. I don't want his charity or his obligations. I'm going to sell this place and set up a store. It's an erotic store, I'll do what I'm actually good at, and I already have a unit down the road I've been eyeing up for a while. My father will go mad," he smirked. "You've—" he looked down at her adorably. "You've actually helped a lot in helping me get here, Harper. I owe you my freedom."

"You didn't spend any of the money I tipped you?"

That surprised her. She had always expected Tan to use that money to buy himself nice things. To treat himself, or at least that was half of her intention when she had tipped him. He shook his head but then paused to think.

"Well, except for these." He pointed to each of his nipples and her eyes closed momentarily as she thought about getting him naked. How could she do it without him thinking her to be some insatiable little thing? She was obsessed with him, even now. More so now, if it was possible. "And this."

He began to unbutton his shirt, shrugging off his slate grey blazer to the floor, and she bit her lip. It was as though he could read her mind, thank God for that.

With his shirt off, she took in the expanse of his tattoos that littered his strong, toned chest. They all mixed into one and she hadn't had much time to truly look at them last night. There was a snowy-haired fox on his left pec, a boa constrictor snake winding down his abdomen and underneath his belt. But he pointed his finger to a small tattoo right by his ribs.

Bending her head, she pushed his finger to the side where it covered the tattoo he was trying to show her. He smiled and lifted his head as she perused his chest. A little book with a small worm travelling through it laid between his pecs, right over his heart.

"When—" she choked up. "When did you get this?"

"Around the time I found out who you were. The first time you tipped me over £100. I was surprised, to say the least, so I got this for you."

"That was the day of your birthday, Atlas! Back in June! Three months ago!"

She crushed her forehead to his chest, letting out a little moan as she hid away from her embarrassment at him having known her identity for so long.

"Yeah, it's been hard to keep it in, now that you mention it. I just thought I would make your life a little more hellish at work and you'd reveal yourself to me. So that I could do what I wanted to you, finally. But no, you had to be hard work, didn't you, baby?"

She nodded her head, smiling softly up at him.

"I didn't know you knew my birthday..." he said gently.

"We've worked together a long time. It's not as though I've never noticed things about you."

"I know that you take your tea with three sugars. Like a crazy person," he laughed and she patted his chest lightly in admonishment.

"You like to blast out music at your desk through your headphones. Drove me up the wall," she added.

"Yeah? Well you wear these ridiculously tight skirts that show off your ass so fucking amazingly that I had to excuse myself to the bathroom whenever you'd wear them."

Her jaw dropped.

"That's why you always used to get up from your seat whenever I'd come into work wearing them?"

He nodded.

"I thought you hated them or something. Thought you were annoyed with me."

"You're deluded. I found it hard enough to sit by you anyway, knowing what a good girl you had been for me the night before during my stream. When you told me you bought that dildo—" he cut himself off and bit his lip. "I was off work for a few days, you remember? I knew I wouldn't be able to sit next to you, knowing how hard you'd fucked yourself with it for me. Wanted to give you the real thing even then."

Her breathing had become erratic and his lips were now so close to hers that her eyelashes fluttered closed at the feeling.

"What made you think to give me a private show? To invite me here?"

"I got tired of waiting. I needed you," he mumbled against her lips before pressing his firmly against them. Atlas hoisted her up to straddle his waist and immediately pushed her back up against the wall beside them so that he could delve his tongue into her open mouth. His kiss was impatient, desperate and just what she needed it to be. It drove her forward, deepening it, making sure he knew that she wanted him. All of him. That she appreciated everything he'd done for her, even if he had taken the long, difficult road to do it.

"I can't wait now," she whispered between breaths.

"Mmm," he whined. "But I like working you up, baby."

"Next time," she promised. "I need you now, Atlas."

He grunted, pulling down his trousers with one hand and letting his thick cock spring free. It pushed against her thighs when he pulled down the stockings she'd worn beneath her dress, giving him access to her already sopping wet pussy.

"My name sounds so good on your tongue. Did you ever scream it? When you came? Just once?" He asked desperately, pulling her panties to the side so that he could feel how wet she was for him. He needn't bother, she thought, she was always ready to take his cock inside of her.

"Just once," she panted against his neck, her fingers clinging to his previously styled blond hair. Madeline couldn't get enough of feeling his smooth skin and soft hair beneath her hands, never having to imagine it again. Her was hers, always had been. But now it was real and electrifying and so, so right.

"That's not nearly enough, baby. Let me change that."

His deep, rumbling voice cracked with a sharp inhale as he pushed his long, hard cock through her wetness. All the way until he settled in deep, holding himself there while she bit down on her lower lip at the stretch of him.

"I'll never get enough of you," he growled, pressing laving hot kisses against her pulse point, taking her breath away.

"Show me," she pleaded. "Atlas, please."

And he did. Repeatedly. Passionately.

The first time that day was right there against his the wall beside his bedroom, too impatient to go inside and fuck on his bed. The sound of skin slapping against skin had filled the hallways and Madeline had wasted no time in coming all over his cock before he followed, his come sliding down her thighs onto the floor.

The second time was after he'd been eyeing up her legs once she'd stepped out of the shower. He'd pushed her back inside underneath the hot spray of water, made her suck his cock down her throat and bounced her arse against him while holding her hands against the shower wall. She had needed another shower afterwards.

The third time, he'd demanded that she ride his face when they'd settled into bed for the night. Having no experience of a man ever requesting this of her, Madeline was understandably a little anxious. But the way he looked at her as he spread his long, tattooed limbs across the bed made her want to give him whatever he asked for.

"You want me to sit on your face?"

He pumped his achingly sore cock at the base, his face straining with the need to come.

"Please. Fuck— baby, please. Don't just sit on it. Fucking smother me. You know how much I love this ass," he said, spanking her hard once.

She gasped and gritted her teeth at the sting.

That was it, she thought. If he wanted her to ride his face, if he wanted her to near-about suffocate him underneath her, she would.

"Fine!" She said, crawling up his body, watching the way he observed her with awe before she settled herself over his face. He licked his lips and pumped his cock harder just as her slick folds made contact with his hot mouth.

His tongue felt so good against her clit that she wanted to just stay there, hovering above him, but he had made her come four times already that day and she needed to balance the books.

"More," he mumbled and she took that as instruction enough to lower her thick thighs down to rest on his chest, her plump arse cheeks covering his mouth and nose.

"Mmm,' he groaned loudly from underneath her, licking his way from her cunt, dipping inside of her for a second, all the way up to her puckered hole. She gasped as he licked and sucked at her crevice, bringing one hand up to squeeze at her right cheek, pulling her down further.

Madeline was shocked at how long he stayed this way with her practically cutting off his air supply before he lifted her up slightly to take a deep inhale.

"Fuck, such a good girl. You're going to make me come if you do that again—"

His praise had always wanted her to give him more, use him more and to do as he said but the thought that she could get him off from squashing him beneath her thick thighs and ass was new. And she wanted to see how long he would last so she cut him off by lowering herself back down unceremoniously, without warning.

As it turned out, he didn't last long at all which made her very happy.

Atlas bit down upon the fleshy part of her arse as he pumped the reddened head of his cock, spurting his come across himself and, as he bucked his hips, a little reached her face, landing on her lower lip.

Her mouth fell open as she watched him in all his sexual majesty. He was incredible and she would never tire of him, she knew.

Where Madeline thought that it would be her to be the one to always get fucked incomprehensible, it seemed she had found Atlas' weakness.

"I—fuck— what— baby—" he babbled, his eyes squeezed shut as his hips bucked again, repeatedly, while his orgasm drew out.

"I'll be doing that again," she giggled, biting her lip and climbing off of him.

He smacked her ass one more time as she did so.

"Yes," he panted. "Everyday. Every goddamned day."

When he opened his eyes to look at her, he smirked and pulled her down to lay beside him.

"You've got a little something on your lip. Let me clean it off for you."

Atlas proceeded to set her heart racing for what felt like the hundredth time that day as they celebrated their futures. Both together and separately. He licked her lip slowly, catching his own release, before kissing her with abandon, tasting her and himself on his tongue.

After a thorough make-out session to close off her day - she was utterly exhausted from what was a highly emotional, draining but spectacular day - whereby Atlas teased every moan he could from her lips, they settled into bed together for the first time properly.

Yeah, she thought as she began to drift off tangled up in his arms, she would never tire of this.

Epilogue - 2 Months Later

"Well it's taken you long enough," Dahlia said when Madeline finally announced that, not only had she had sex for the first time in over a year, but that she had a boyfriend. "When am I meeting him?"

The woman raised a black, slender eyebrow as though she was preparing herself to judge and criticise every inch of whoever it was that had stolen Madeline's heart. Dahlia was protective at the best of times.

"He's just getting our drinks," Madeline laughed.

When Atlas strode over, wearing an open-chested white shirt, black leather jacket and tight black jeans with thick army boots, Dahlia jaw dropped to the floor. He had styled his platinum blond hair messily and greeted her with that beaming smile that always knocked Madeline senseless.

Recovering herself, Dahlia muttered, "Turn around", whilst spinning a finger in his direction. No 'hello'. No 'nice to meet you'. It seemed her best friend and boyfriend were on somewhat of a similar wavelength in terms of their politeness.

Atlas sighed, winking to Madeline as he turned to face her. Dahlia's face gave nothing away as she took him in until his back was directed at her.

'Oh my god, nice!' Dahlia mouthed to Madeline, forcing her to bite her lip at the praise. If she liked him then she knew there would be no issue with her other friends.

"Do I get your seal of approval?" He drawled as he completed his 180 degree spin.

"You'll do," she mused, picking up her drink.

"I was just saying to Lia, Atlas, that it's been a long time that she's been single."

"Single and thriving, babe," she smiled, bringing her cosmopolitan to her red-stained lips. "I don't need a man."

Madeline didn't seem to think so. Random hookup after random hookup. A string of men falling at her feet. Dahlia liked to keep them on the chain but never progress anywhere with any of them. And she suspected it was because she wasn't looking in the right place. Always going for the guy who wanted to fuck and chuck her, claiming that's what she wanted too. But Madeline saw through that. It wasn't difficult. The woman was so in-need of love, it hurt her that she couldn't find it.

"What's your usual type?" Atlas asked and felt the eyes of his girlfriend's best friend travel down his body. He raised an eyebrow in surprise before looking over to Madeline for help.

"You leave him alone. He's mine. God knows I waited long enough for him."

The raven-haired woman sighed and said, "Fine. Got any friends, Atlas?"

"I do," he drawled after taking a sip of his whisky.

"Any of 'em tall?"

"Yes, a few."

"Muscular? I like them big," she said, emphasising her meaning with her hands.

"There's one that's bigger than me, actually."

Dahlia's eyebrows shot to the roof, her interest severely piqued though she was trying to keep herself looking cool.

"But he might not be for you," Atlas teased and watched Dahlia's lips curve into a frown. "So again, what's your type?"

"Horny," Madeline joked and received a quick elbow to the ribs from her best friend. "Ow! Tell me I'm wrong!"

"In that case, he's perfect. He's actually a pornstar."

"Oh yes!" Madeline exclaimed. "Hollis would be perfect for—"

"Excuse me?" Dahlia chimed in, flicking her long hair over her shoulder. "His name is Hollis?"

"Yes, is that a problem?" Atlas asked.

"He sounds stuffy but...," she chirped, standing from her seat. "Send me a link to his stuff. I like to window shop before I buy."

With that, the woman walked off towards the bar, shaking her hips in that way that she did when she knew an attractive man was watching. Lo and behold, she only had chance to take a seat on the barstool for ten seconds before a man approached her, eyeing her up like she was cotton candy.

"That was easier than I thought. You'd better send her that link tonight or else I'll never hear the end of it," Madeline laughed.

"He's going to kill me before she can kill him. Now, Bookworm, why don't we get you home?" Atlas said, his eyes dipping to the low cut neckline of Madeline's dress.

She nodded, biting her lip, "I have a surprise for you tonight."

After Atlas had resigned from the cleric's office, the two of them had spent a lot of time together. Talking. Fucking. Cuddling. All of it. But after a couple of weeks, Madeline's post as Councilwoman had begun and they had run out of spare time.

The routine had been similar to how it'd always been before they'd gotten together; Madeline would work the early shift, go back to her apartment to eat and then tune into TitanVideo's stream. It was hotter, in a way, watching her boyfriend on the screen now than before. When he would wink into the camera, she knew it was for her. And when he said 'goodnight' in that seductive, low register, shivers passed up her spine at the memory of every time he'd done that to her whilst lying in bed together.

It drove her mad though, all the same.

She told herself that she wanted this. Wanted the separation a little bit. The freedom to come and go as she pleased. To see him properly at the weekends. He was busy trying to sell his apartment to find one a little smaller, cheaper and more manageable whilst he ran his store.

The store, Titan Erotics, was a raging success. All of his subscribers had flocked there on the opening day and bought something. They were regular visitors. Madeline suspected that it was mostly to see him, rather than his product line, but it didn't bother her. If she wasn't his girlfriend, she would have done the same thing. He wore his skull and crossbones mask while he worked to keep up the illusion, not wanting to reveal too much of himself.

That he reserved only for Madeline.

But after a couple of months of this, of only seeing him at the weekends rather than through her laptop screen, she came up with an idea. A stupid, reckless, ill-thought-out idea that she hoped he'd go along with. He had a proclivity for idiocy when it came to her, after all.

So as they left the bar, saying a quick goodbye to Dahlia who was tongue-deep in some poor bloke's throat, Madeline asked if he would take her back to his place rather than her own.

"Why do you want to go there? It's all packed up in boxes."

Madeline rolled her eyes and tugged him by the hand into the nearest taxi. Entering his apartment, she dragged him up every flight of stairs, his eyes firmly locked on her behind the whole way up, and into his loft. His camera, spotlight, armchair and bed remained in place as she knew they would be.

"I have a surprise for you."

"Baby, you know I can't handle surprises. Tell me," he bit his lip, pulling her closer into him by her arse.

She smiled and pulled out a thin bit of material from her handbag. Madeline had looked long and hard for something that would be suitable until she finally found the mask just for her in a little corner bookshop.

She tied the bookworm printed mask around her face, pulling it tightly at the back.

Atlas cocked his head to the side as he took her in, registering her meaning.

"You want to join me? On my stream?"

She nodded and began to undress him, taking off his jacket first followed by his shirt. When she reached his buckle, she took her time in slowly unclasping it, watching his eyes darken as he stared into hers.

"Why is it turning me on so much that I can only see your eyes?"

Madeline looked up at him beneath her heavy lids, giving him her best impression of siren eyes that she could.

"Now you know how mad you drove me," she breathed, excited to get him naked. "Turn it on."

He moved towards the camera, alerted his fans to his upcoming stream and removed his trousers the rest of the way.

Her eyes danced over his body when she realised he hadn't worn any boxers to the bar, his cock springing free against his stomach.

"Baby, I swear if you don't get out of that dress now, you'll be losing another one."

She licked her lips, eager to watch his desperation grow for her as she pulled the straps down her shoulders and let the material fall to the floor at her feet.

"Fuck," he moaned, taking her in, and his cock bobbed, growing harder at the sight of her. "I can't wait to see what my viewers suggest for us tonight, Bookworm."

Atlas placed his mask over his face, sat down in the armchair and pulled Madeline onto his lap, sucking one of her stiff nipples into his mouth just as the red light blinked on his camera.

They were live. Madeline's core clenched in anticipation.

"Evening," he began in that voice that made her want to let him breed her. "Bookworm will be joining us again tonight and, if you like her, maybe I'll keep her. How does that sound?"

Messages began to fill the chat:

She's back! Fuck, it was so hot last time.

TIP! £80 - Oh this is going to be good.

TIP! £100 - Tan, fuck that whore for me.

Since Madeline's last appearance on TitanVideo's livestream, he had gained a flood of new subscribers. Many more men had signed up to watch him. Atlas already had a large gay following which he was immensely proud of but these new viewers wanted to watch for an altogether different reason. It was half of the reason that she'd decided to gatecrash his show tonight.

"I think you should do as they say, Tan," Madeline said in her most seductive voice. She hoped it would work on Atlas to push him closer to the edge at least if not their watchers but judging by the way he bucked his hips underneath her, she knew it had affected him.

"I'll do what I like with you," he said, gritting his teeth as he pinched her cheeks together.

Oh, she loved when he became like this. Hard. Stern. Possessive. With the jump in straight men that had begun to tune into his livestreams, so had come the requests - crude as they had been - for him to bring Bookworm back. And with them their desire to watch him fuck her silly. Watching on from home, she had encouraged it, told those viewers that she would love to be fucked raw for their pleasure by Tan. That's when she had discovered that Atlas was exhibiting the signs of Xelophilia. He was getting off on his jealousy, pumping his pierced length harder at watching her flirt over the airwaves with his subscribers.

And they had loved every second of it. So had she.

"They want to see you take me, Tan. Why don't you be a man and do it? Or else, maybe I should take up one of their offers to sit in their lap instead," she teased.

"As you command," he growled, looking directly into the camera. "But first, you're getting whipped for speaking out of turn."

Her eyes went wide as Atlas picked her up over his shoulder, spanking her once in full view of the camera, before placing her over the back of the armchair. He held her down with one large, firm hand to her lower back, while he fetched a long, thin paddle from a box by his feet.

She was dripping wet already, her slick cunt on display deliciously. Madeline tried to turn, to look over her shoulder and see what he was doing but it was no use. She was trying desperately hard not to fall over the side entirely with the way that he had positioned her; arse up and legs spread.

"Apologise and I'll put this away," he offered, being more generous than if they were alone.

"Fuck you," she spat, wanting nothing more than the punishment he was going to dole out to her.

"Don't say I didn't warn you," his voice strained as he smacked the paddle down onto her right arse cheek, leaving a thick red mark that she knew would bruise. "Count, whore."

Her eyes rolled back in her head as a whimper left her throat at the combined smack and his filthy words.

"One."

He brought it down again on the same cheek, making her keen with the sting.

"Two."

"How many slaps should I give her, guys?" Atlas asked, doling out another and ripping a throaty yell from her lips.

"Three!"

She prayed he would swap cheeks next time, just for a momentary reprieve but he didn't. That paddle, which she had no regrets about buying from his store on its opening day, would be put to good use that night, she thought. There was no way that he would let her get off easily and he smacked her for a fourth time without even reading the messages flocking through, meaning she wasn't even close to finished with her punishment yet.

"Four! Ah!"

Atlas chuckled darkly in her ear as he walked around her, smacking her a fifth time on the same cheek with his hand this time, leaving a white outline of his fingers on her reddened arse.

"Five," she cried.

He stared down at her for a moment, ignoring his fan's pleas, to whisper, "I can't fucking wait to get inside you, baby. You're so wet for me."

"Please," Madeline whimpered, her juices spilling down her thighs.

"Oh no, not just yet. We haven't given the people what they want yet. And how many slaps does this slut deserve?" He raised his voice as he moved over to the laptop where he read message after message flooding the chat. "Ohhh, yes. Bookworm, you'd better get yourself comfortable. They want twenty," he smirked devilishly.

Her eyes shot wide and she tried to get up, tried to run away and she almost managed it - always loved role-playing this way with him so that Atlas would have to scoop her up - but he'd caught her. Like he always did. But then she didn't ever try too hard, hoping he would bring her right back right where she belonged.

Atlas proceeded to paddle her arse over the back of his armchair until she'd screamed twenty times, her clit rubbing on the nubbed hem at the top of it, until the ecstasy of being reprimanded over and over caught up with her. She did as she was told when he whispered a sinful, "Come," in her ear, hardly able to hold back any longer. Her thighs were covered with her own release and she was starting to feel over-sensitive when Atlas lifted up his mask to lick her clean between her thighs.

"Fuckmefuckmefuckmefuckme," she begged and was only met with Atlas' teasing laugh.

"This whore wants to get fucked, guys. Think she deserves this cock?" He asked, squeezing the base of his length. She knew he must have been desperate for it too. He was usually all for getting right to it when she asked, not one to refuse her, unless he'd decided he wanted to hear her sweet begging, but she knew this was all for the show. And she fucking loved it.

"Fortunately for you, baby, they want to see this pussy stretched. Get up," he commanded and she did so to the best of her ability on shaky legs.

Atlas sat down in the armchair and patted his thigh, beckoning her over. She bit her lip hard, staring at his leaking tip and her mouth ran dry at the sight of him. Thick and long and ready to ruin her.

"I won't ask again, Bookworm. Sit down on me or don't," he smirked, teasing, torturing.

Madeline rushed to sit down on his lap, her back pulled flush to his chest as he reached a hand up to cup one of her breasts. He slapped the tip of his cock against her swollen clit once, twice, a third time and she became ravenous for him to be inside of her so took matters into her own hands. Madeline gripped the base of him hard, just as he always liked, and slowly lined him up with her wet core before she sat down on him all at once. The hand cupping her quickly moved to pinch her tight nipple hard and she screamed as he did so, feeling overwhelmed with intense pleasure and pain hitting her body simultaneously.

Running a hand up her chest and neck, Atlas pulled her face towards him so that he could place a kiss against her mask just over her lips.

She whimpered, needing to feel his kiss properly. This way, she couldn't feel the outline of his full lips or the wetness of his tongue.

"It's not nice to be teased, is it, baby? This is the only type of kiss you're getting tonight so that you learn your lesson for pulling the same stunt on me."

She panted into his neck, clutching tightly on the armrests of the chair as he pounded his hips up against her.

"No," she whined. "Please. I'm sorry."

"Sorry doesn't cut it, Councilwoman," he whispered to avoid it being picked up by his mic. Her eyes rolled back at the use of her title. The man just couldn't resist giving her another kink to work into their sessions.

"Please. Touch my clit, I need—"

Don't do it, Tan, make her beg.

Fuck, this is so hot.

TIP! £100 - Let her come on your cock.

"Sorry, baby. They don't want me to help you. Come on, I know you can take just this cock. You don't need anything else," he panted, getting perilously close to his own high.

"I can't, I need something—"

Atlas began to thrust in and out of her so quickly, pushing up against her inner walls so expertly that she thought she would black out entirely. But something was missing and she couldn't think what.

"How about this? Be quiet and they won't notice. They want to edge you, Darling, but consider me a gracious master, yeah?" His deep voice rumbled in her ear as he pushed a finger into his mouth, wetting it thoroughly, and then pressed it roughly against her puckered virgin hole, pushing inside.

"Oh, fuck!" She cried and it only took three more thrusts in both of her holes for her to tip over the edge. Her head slammed back against his chest while he held her firmly in place, one hand cupping her jaw, and followed her, coming deep inside of her spent cunt.

He was a gracious master indeed.

"At— Atla—" she began to babble, bucking her hips with the pleasure still coasting through every nerve ending in her body. He quickly lifted his hand to her mouth, covering it and shutting her up to prevent anyone hearing his name fall from her lips.

"As much as I love hearing you cry my name, you need to be careful, baby, huh?"

Giving her the benefit of the doubt after she nodded her head in agreement, Atlas removed his hand from her lips and pulled himself out of her, his flaccid cock lying against his thigh.

Madeline, in another world - one of bliss and pleasure and him - couldn't help the words she'd wanted to say for two months from slipping out of her mouth. Unfortunately for her, it was unwittingly incomprehensible and during one of Atlas' most popular streams of all time.

"I— Atlas— I lov—" she began and he covered her mouth back up before registering what she was about to say.

"Wait, what?" He whispered in an attempt to keep her words private.

"I love you," she said, her eyes shut tight as she rested momentarily against his chest.

Pinging noises originating from the laptop were ceaseless as their viewers praised them for the show, sending more requests for what they wanted to see next. But all Atlas could think about was her words. Those three words that he'd wanted to say for longer than two months. For over a year since he'd become besotted with the swotty, argumentative woman from his office.

The smile on his face stretched wide, his dimples coming out in full force, and he wiped his eyes in disbelief, pulling his arms so tight around the woman he wanted for life.

"I love you too, Darling," he spoke so gently in her ear.

She smiled in response, coming back to the present, and opened her eyes to look at him. She wished she could see his face properly, count those freckles on his nose as they scrunched up with his gleeful expression.

But she could have that later. Could have him for as long as she wanted. And as far as Madeline was concerned, there was no end in sight. She didn't want the man in her life to leave her alone as she used to. She didn't want space away from him. She wanted all of him, body, soul and mind.

"Come and live with me," she asked, kissing his sharp jaw as she rested on his lap, tucked safely in the comfort of his arms.

"Come— come and live with you? I have a little place I was looking at by the store. About to put an offer on it."

She shook her head and frowned.

"My place is closer."

Well he couldn't argue with that. But truth be told, he wouldn't have cared if her apartment was fifty miles away. If she wanted him, he wouldn't refuse her. Couldn't ever.

"Okay," he beamed and she promised she would kiss him properly in the full magnitude that the situation commanded later.

For now, they still had a show to do.

Madeline stood from his lap and stretched out her arm to help him up.
"Now that we've done what the men in the chat want to do, I think it's time we listened to what our female audience want, Tan," she said, louder so that their audience could hear them properly.

"I like the way you think, Bookworm. What do you want, ladies? Lay it on me. Like I said, I'm nothing if not adventurous," he said, winking at Madeline over his shoulder.

Atlas' face turned ashen and she bit her lip with excitement when the messages came through.

"Oh, wait…" he started, having read the popular vote.

She bent down to retrieve the items she would need to fulfil their viewers' request from the box sitting by the armchair.

"All talk are you, baby?" She teased, walking towards him with a harness and her Tan-sized dildo.

Atlas' jaw fell before he clenched his teeth together, looking from the camera to Madeline and back again. The stain on his cheeks was adorable and she had always dreamed of seeing him flustered like this. Just like he had done to her so many times over. Her blood ran hot at the prospect that it was now her turn.

She strapped the dildo to her waist, preparing herself for something incredible.

"What's your colour?" She asked.

It didn't even take him a moment, surprising her, for him to say, "Green."

"You're sure?" She asked again, giving him the opportunity to back out one last time.

Taking her in, Atlas' eyes darkened, he wet his lips and grumbled, "Bring it on, baby."

Don't miss out!

Visit the website below and you can sign up to receive emails whenever Ivy Ingle-Moss publishes a new book. There's no charge and no obligation.

https://books2read.com/r/B-A-TXJSB-DXWPD

BOOKS 2 READ

Connecting independent readers to independent writers.